When You Were Born...

Emma Dodd

When you were born
the rain stopped,

the sun came out,
the sky turned blue.

When you were born
the snow melted,

the birds sang,
the flowers grew.

When you were born
the grass sighed,

the ocean sparkled,
a breeze blew.

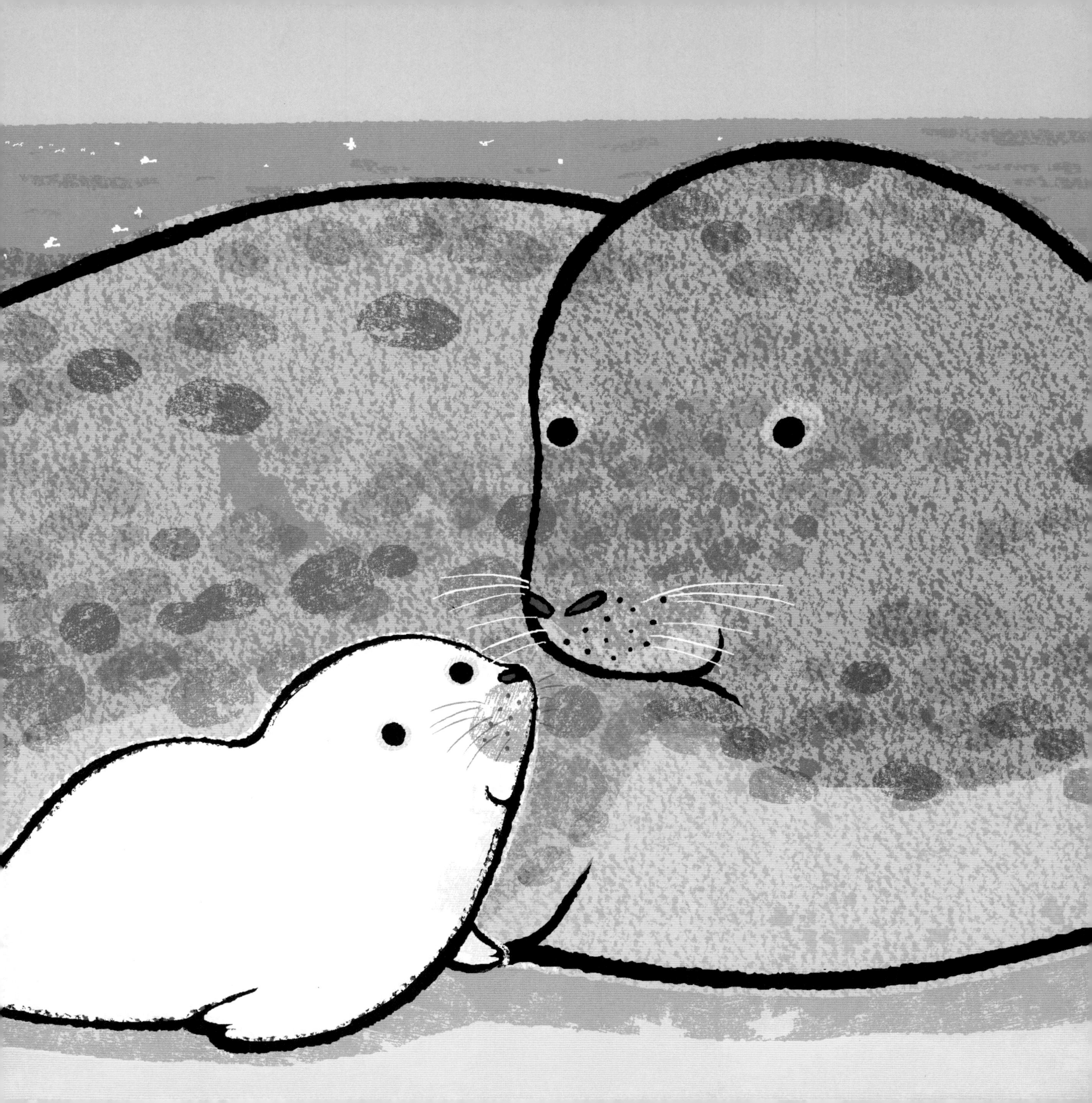

When you were born
our hearts sang,

our spirits soared,
our troubles flew.

When you were born
we all laughed,

we all cried,
our dreams came true.

When you were born
our eyes saw
the world anew.

A TEMPLAR BOOK

First published in the UK in 2013 by Templar Publishing
This softback edition published in 2014 by Templar Publishing,
an imprint of The Templar Company Limited,
Deepdene Lodge, Deepdene Avenue, Dorking, Surrey, RH5 4AT
www.templarco.co.uk

1 3 5 7 9 10 8 6 4 2

ISBN: 978-1-78370-099-8

Printed in China